**ALICIA DURAN**
has a BA in Spanish Language and Literature from
Bryn Mawr College and an MA in International
Affairs from Columbia University. She works in
children's publishing in New Jersey.

**BRIAN FITZGERALD**
is an internationally recognized, award-winning
illustrator who lives and works in Ireland.

*Apple Pie Picnic*
Text copyright © 2023 Alicia Duran
Illustrations copyright © 2023 Brian Fitzgerald
Published in 2023 by Red Comet Press, LLC, Brooklyn, NY

Library of Congress Control Number: 2022941199

ISBN (HB): 978-1-63655-061-9
ISBN (EBOOK): 978-1-63655-062-6

22 23 24 25 TLF 10 9 8 7 6 5 4 3 2 1

First Edition
Manufactured in China

RED COMET ● PRESS
RedCometPress.com

# APPLE PiE PiCNIC

ALICIA DURAN     BRIAN FITZGERALD

RED COMET PRESS ● BROOKLYN

This is the apple tree, *el manzano*,
that grows near the house where
Rosa lives.

The is the sun, *el sol*,
that shines every day
on the tree near the house.

This is the rain, *la lluvia*,
that soaks the leaves and branches
and feeds the apple tree
near the house where Rosa lives.

These are the birds, *los pájaros*,
that build a nest in the tree.

This is the cat, *el gato*,
who tries to creep close to the nest,
built by birds on a high branch,
which grows on the tree
near the house where Rosa lives.

This is Rosa's dog, *el perro*,
who chases away the cat,
which helps the bird in her nest.

These are the flowers, *las flores*,
that bloom every spring on the tree
near the house where Rosa lives
with her family and her pets.

These are the bees, *las abejas*,
that buzz from flower to flower,
pollinating the blossoms so they can grow fruit.

And this is Churro,
getting stung by a bee.
Ouch!

This is the special resting spot
that Rosa found in the crack of the tree,
el *árbol*, which grows near her house.

These are the squirrels,
who scurry up and down the tree
near the house where Rosa lives.

This is the little girl, *la niña*, Rosa, climbing up to her resting spot, while Churro points his nose up as if to say, "Take me with you!"

And this is Dulce, the cat,
climbing up the trunk of the tree
near the house where Rosa lives.

The warm days of spring, *la primavera*, pass by as Rosa watches the apple blossoms slowly turn into fruits.

These are the small apples, *las manzanas*,
which emerge from the blossoms,
pollinated by bees, who buzz from branch to branch
on the tree that grows near Rosa's house.

These are the apples—red, ripe, and ready—
that grow in the rain beneath the sun's rays,
on the tree near the house where Rosa lives.

And this is Rosa, who climbs to her special spot
in the crook of the old apple tree,
saying to the bugs and the squirrels,
"See this manzana? It's mine!"

This is the raccoon,
who comes out at night, *la noche*,
to eat the ripe apples and gets a surprise!

"Arf-arf!" barks Churro,
who scares the raccoon away from the apples,
hanging ripe and ready on the tree
near the house where Rosa sleeps.

This is Rosa's grandmother, *la abuela*, filling baskets with red apples picked by Rosa's family, *la familia*.

This is Rosa's mother, *la madre*,
carrying the fruit, plucked from
the tree near the house where Rosa lives.

This is Rosa's grandfather, *el abuelo*, making a crusty pie from the ripe apples that were picked from the apple tree.

And this is Rosa,
packing the picnic basket,
which she will carry to a shady spot
under the big, old apple tree.

This is la familia,
spreading the blanket,
unpacking the basket,
sharing the food and the
fun beneath the shade of the
apple tree that grows near
the house where they live.

This is the apple tree that grows
near the house where Rosa lives,
getting ready for a long winter's nap.

# FROM FLOWER TO FRUIT

Once apple blossoms (flowers)
are pollinated by bees,
the fruits begin to grow.

The time from flower to
fruit is four to six months.
(For example, April,
May, June, July,
August, September . . .)

Ripe apples are harvested from late summer until fall.

Apples can be kept in storage for months— as long as it is not too cold and not too hot.

It takes four to five years for apple trees to grow up and produce fruit.

# ENGLISH AND SPANISH WORDS

tree/árbol

grandfather/
abuelo

grandmother/
abuela

mother/madre

girl/niña

male cat/gato
female cat/gata

male dog/perro
female dog/perra

bird/pájaro
apple/manzana

# APPLE SAUCE

It's hard to make apple pie,
but it's easy to make applesauce.

Start with six apples. Two different kinds are good. Have a grown-up cut the apples into quarters. Then you can cut the apples into smaller pieces.

Measure sugar—about one-half a cup; water—about 2 cups; cinnamon—about 1 teaspoon; butter—about 1 tablespoon.

Put everything in a heavy saucepan and have a grown-up cook the apples until they are soft and foamy—about 20 minutes.

Let the apples cool. Add some strawberries or raspberries for color.

If you like your applesauce smooth (not lumpy), mash it with a potato masher or a fork once it is at room temperature.